Put Beginning Readers on the Right Track with
ALL ABOARD READING™

The All Aboard Reading series is especially for beginning readers. Written by noted authors and illustrated in full color, these are books that children really and truly *want* to read—books to excite their imagination, tickle their funny bone, expand their interests, and support their feelings. With four different reading levels, All Aboard Reading lets you choose which books are most appropriate for your children and their growing abilities.

Picture Readers—for Ages 3 to 6
Picture Readers have super-simple texts, with many nouns appearing as rebus pictures. At the end of each book are 24 flash cards—on one side is the rebus picture; on the other side is the written-out word.

Level 1—for Preschool through First-Grade Children
Level 1 books have very few lines per page, very large type, easy words, lots of repetition, and pictures with visual "cues" to help children figure out the words on the page.

Level 2—for First-Grade to Third-Grade Children
Level 2 books are printed in slightly smaller type than Level 1 books. The stories are more complex, but there is still lots of repetition in the text, and many pictures. The sentences are quite simple and are broken up into short lines to make reading easier.

Level 3—for Second-Grade through Third-Grade Children
Level 3 books have considerably longer texts, harder words, and more complicated sentences.

All Aboard for happy reading!

D1165194

To Clyde Robert Bulla—Stephanie Spinner

Text copyright © 1999 by Stephanie Spinner. Illustrations copyright © 1999 by Susan Swan.
All rights reserved. Published by Grosset & Dunlap, Inc., a member of Penguin Putnam Books
for Young Readers, New York. ALL ABOARD READING is a trademark of The Putnam &
Grosset Group. GROSSET & DUNLAP is a trademark of Grosset & Dunlap, Inc. Published
simultaneously in Canada. Printed in the U.S.A.

Library of Congress Cataloging-in-Publication Data

Spinner, Stephanie.
    Snake hair ; the story of Medusa / by Stephanie Spinner ; illustrated by Susan Swan.
        p.   cm. — (All aboard reading. Level 2)
    Summary: Recounts how the Greek hero Perseus vanquished the serpent-haired Medusa
whose gaze turned people to stone.
    1. Medusa (Greek mythology)—Juvenile literature. 2. Perseus (Greek mythology)—
Juvenile literature. [1. Medusa (Greek mythology) 2. Perseus (Greek mythology) 3.
Mythology, Greek.] I. Swan, Susan Elizabeth, ill. II. Title. III. Series.
BL820.M38S65   1999
398.2'0938'02—dc21   98-54663
                                                                                                                            CIP
ISBN 0-448-42049-X (GB) A B C D E F G H I J   AC

ISBN 0-448-41981-5 (pbk.) A B C D E F G H I J

ALL
ABOARD
READING™

Level 2
Grades 1-3

Snake Hair
The Story of Medusa

By Stephanie Spinner
Illustrated by Susan Swan

Grosset & Dunlap • New York

Once there was a young girl
named Medusa.
(You say it like this: meh-DOO-sa.)
She lived in Greece a long, long time ago.
Medusa was young and pretty.
But she made the gods angry.
This is her story.

Medusa had long, silky hair.

She was proud of it—too proud.

She brushed it and combed it

all the time.

Then one day she said,

"My hair is more beautiful

than the hair of Athena."

(You say it like this: uh-THEE-na.)

That was a big mistake.

Athena was a powerful goddess.

She heard Medusa's words.

They made her very angry.

"Foolish girl!" said Athena.

"Your words have

cost you your beauty!"

And Athena turned Medusa

into a monster.

Medusa's body was covered with scales.

Her hands were claws.

And her hair—her beautiful hair—

was a swarm of snakes!

She was so ugly that the sight of her

turned people to stone.

Medusa fled to the forest.

She ran and ran.

A deer saw her.

Some rabbits saw her.

In an instant they turned to stone.

One look at her face was all it took.

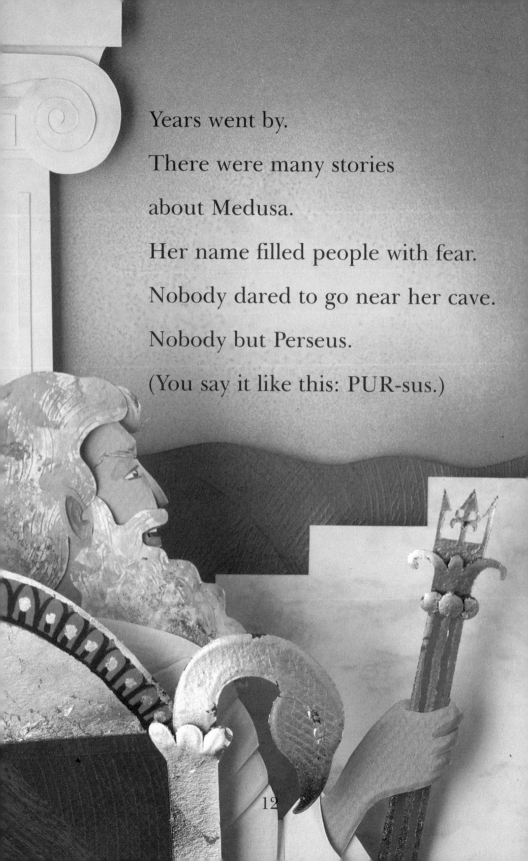

Years went by.

There were many stories

about Medusa.

Her name filled people with fear.

Nobody dared to go near her cave.

Nobody but Perseus.

(You say it like this: PUR-sus.)

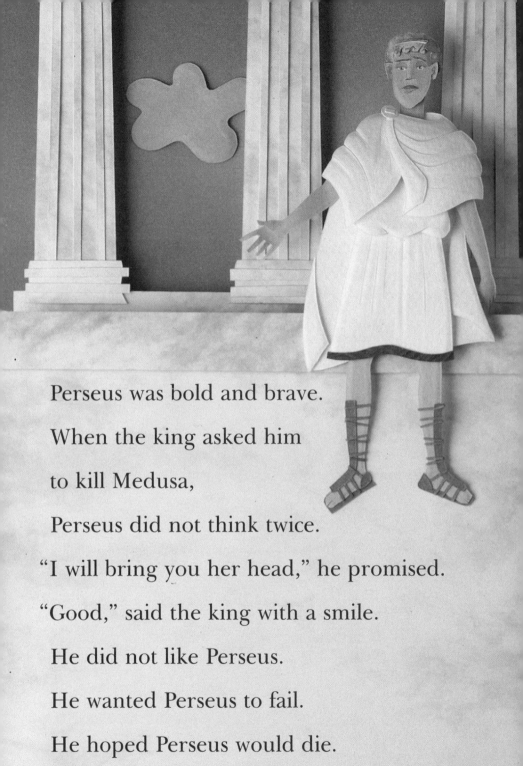

Perseus was bold and brave.

When the king asked him

to kill Medusa,

Perseus did not think twice.

"I will bring you her head," he promised.

"Good," said the king with a smile.

He did not like Perseus.

He wanted Perseus to fail.

He hoped Perseus would die.

Perseus knew the stories

about Medusa.

He did not want to turn to stone.

So he asked the gods to help him.

Athena heard his prayers.

So did Hermes.

(You say it like this: HER-mees.)

Athena gave Perseus a shield.

It was as bright as a mirror.

Hermes gave him shoes with wings.
"These will help you fight Medusa,"
Hermes told him.

Perseus took the shield.

He put on the shoes.

Off he flew.

At last he reached Medusa's cave.

Medusa was sleeping.

Perseus crept into the cave.

He was careful to be quiet.

He did not look at Medusa's face.

But he heard the snakes on her head—

crawling and hissing,

hissing and crawling.

Just then Medusa started to wake.

She began to turn around.

In an instant Perseus would see her face!

Perseus thought quickly.

He raised his shield.

It was as bright as a mirror.

He watched Medusa in it.

Then he raised his sword

and struck her head from her body.

Medusa was dead.

Or was she?

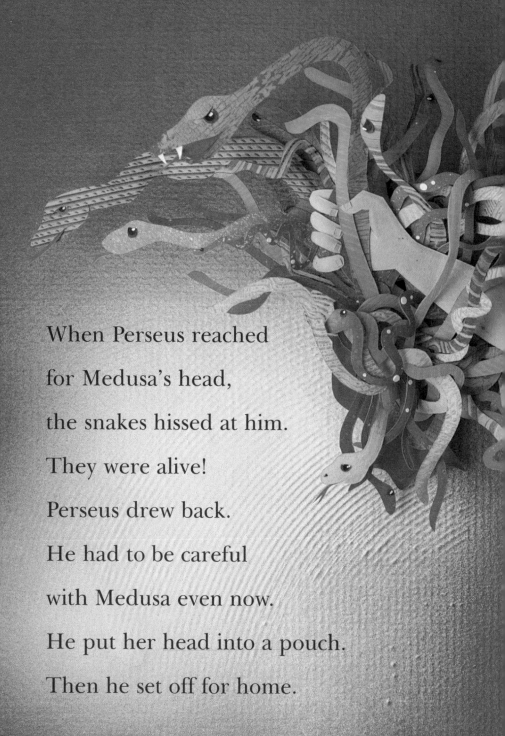

When Perseus reached

for Medusa's head,

the snakes hissed at him.

They were alive!

Perseus drew back.

He had to be careful

with Medusa even now.

He put her head into a pouch.

Then he set off for home.

Perseus flew over the sea.

His adventure was over.

Or so he thought.

But at the edge of the sea

he saw something strange.

He saw a girl chained to a rock.

She was screaming.

Then Perseus saw why.

A giant sea monster

was swimming toward her.

Its jaws were open wide.

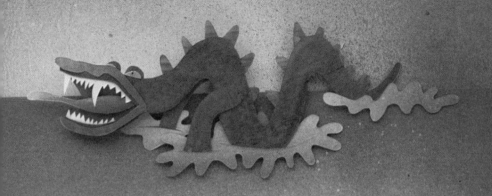

Perseus did not think twice.

He had to save the girl!

He flew down to face the monster.

Its fangs were long.

Its claws were sharp.

But Perseus was not afraid.

"Look away!" he cried to the girl.

She turned her head.

Perseus reached into the pouch.

He pulled out the head of Medusa.

He held it up to the monster.

The snakes crawled and hissed,

hissed and crawled.

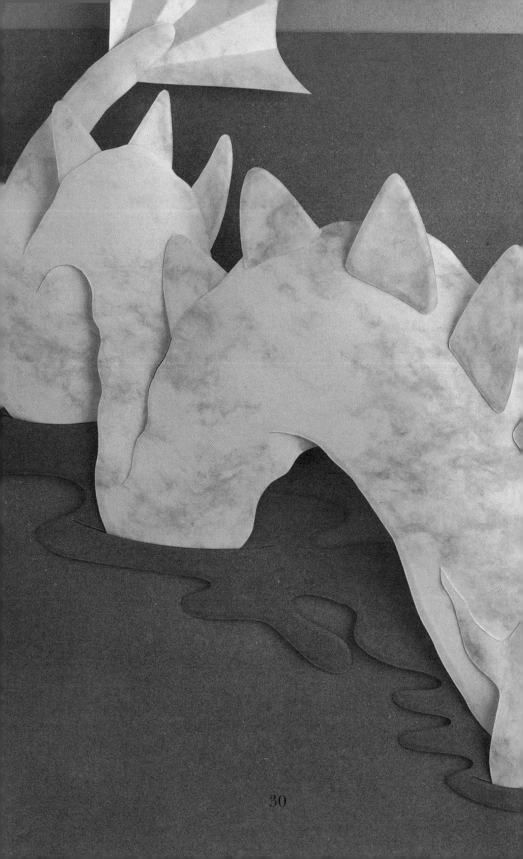

The monster took one look

at Medusa's head

and turned to stone!

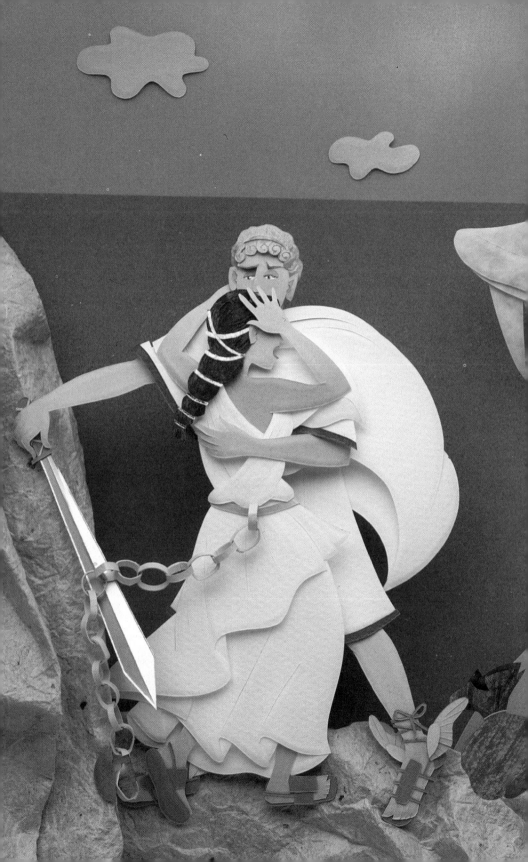

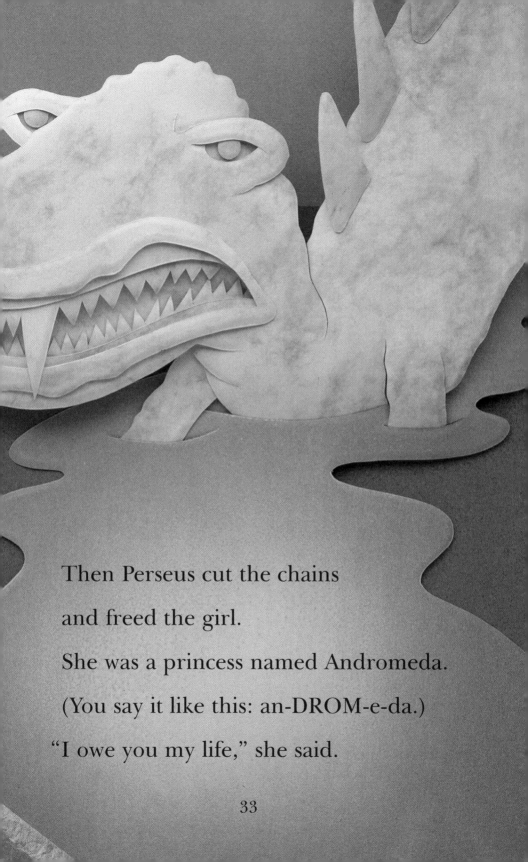

Then Perseus cut the chains
and freed the girl.
She was a princess named Andromeda.
(You say it like this: an-DROM-e-da.)
"I owe you my life," she said.

Perseus returned home with Andromeda.

Then he set off for the palace.

It was time to keep his promise.

It was time to bring the king

the head of Medusa.

On the way he met an old man.

"Beware of the king,"

the old man told him.

"He sent you away

so Medusa would kill you.

He will not be happy to see you alive."

Perseus did not believe the old man.

He walked right into the throne room.

The king saw him and turned pale.

It was as if he were seeing a ghost.

"Why have you come here?"

shouted the king.

"I did not send for you!"

Now Perseus knew that

the old man had been right.

He could not trust the king.

"I kept my word," said Perseus.

"I killed Medusa for you."

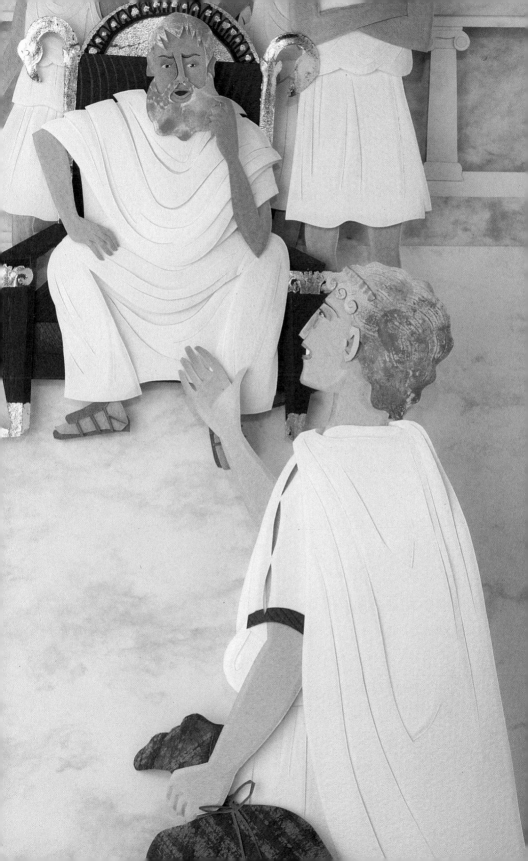

"Liar!" shouted the king.

"Liar!" shouted his men.

They drew their swords.

"If I have any friends here,
let them look away!"
said Perseus.

"I am no liar,"

Perseus said to the king.

"And here is the proof!"

He reached into the pouch.

He pulled out the head of Medusa.

He held it high.

The king and his men

looked at the head.

They saw Medusa's terrible face.

They saw her snaky hair.

And then they saw no more.

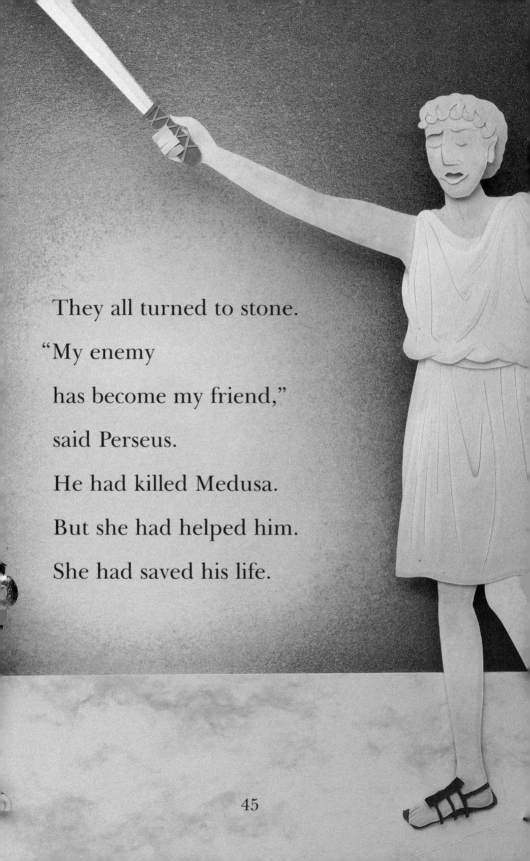

They all turned to stone.

"My enemy

has become my friend,"

said Perseus.

He had killed Medusa.

But she had helped him.

She had saved his life.

After a time,

Perseus became a king.

He married Andromeda.

He ruled his people well.

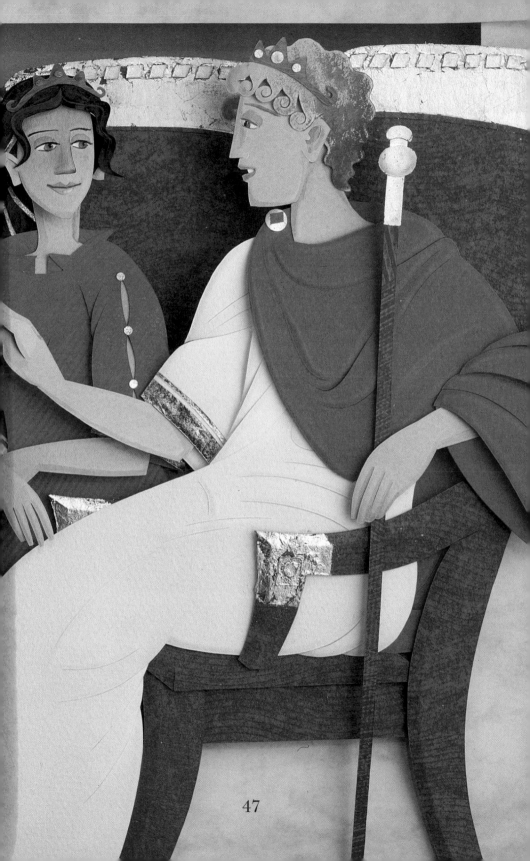

And the head of Medusa?

It was never seen again.